A Night Out with Mama

Quvenzhané Wallis

Illustrated by Vanessa Brantley-Newton

SIMON & SCHUSTER BOOKS FOR YOUNG READERS

NEW YORK   LONDON   TORONTO   SYDNEY   NEW DELHI

SIMON & SCHUSTER BOOKS FOR YOUNG READERS

An imprint of Simon & Schuster Children's Publishing Division • 1230 Avenue of the Americas, New York, New York 10020

Text copyright © 2017 by Jarece Productions, Inc. • Illustrations copyright © 2017 by Vanessa Brantley Newton

All rights reserved, including the right of reproduction in whole or in part in any form. • SIMON & SCHUSTER

BOOKS FOR YOUNG READERS is a trademark of Simon & Schuster, Inc. • For information about special discounts

for bulk purchases, please contact Simon & Schuster Special Sales at 1-866-506-1949 or business@simonandschuster.com.

The Simon & Schuster Speakers Bureau can bring authors to your live event. For more information or to book an event,

contact the Simon & Schuster Speakers Bureau at 1-866-248-3049 or visit our website at www.simonspeakers.com.

Book design by Lucy Ruth Cummins • The text for this book was set in Adobe Caslon Pro.

The illustrations for this book were rendered in Corel Painter.

Manufactured in China • 0717 SCP • First Edition

10 9 8 7 6 5 4 3 2 1

Library of Congress Cataloging-in-Publication Data

Names: Wallis, Quvenzhané, 2003– author. | Brantley-Newton, Vanessa, illustrator.

Title: A night out with Mama /Quvenzhané Wallis ; illustrated by Vanessa Brantley Newton.

Description: First edition. | New York : Simon & Schuster Books for Young Readers, [2017] | Summary:

"A picture book about a little girl who has a big night out with her mother at an awards show"— Provided by publisher.

Identifiers: LCCN 2016020175| ISBN 9781481458801 (hardcover : alk. paper) | ISBN 9781481458818 (ebook)

Subjects: | CYAC: Mothers and daughters—Fiction. | Award presentations—Fiction. | African Americans—Fiction.

Classification: LCC PZ7.1.W357 Ni 2017 | DDC [E]—dc23

LC record available at https://lccn.loc.gov/2016020175

To my parents, for teaching me that
everything is possible —Q. W.

For Zoe and Marley, who wanted to see
brown girls in books —V. B.-N.

My new blue shoes make a soft

tap,

 tap,

  tapping sound
   when I walk
    down the
     hall.

The sun is up now,
and it's just me,
excited for the day
to begin.

Well, just me
and Scruffy. . . .

My sister
wakes first
and then my
brothers.

I tap,
tap,
tap
down the hall.

Finally Mama and Daddy wake up.
"Who's that?" Mama calls out.
"It's just me," I say.

Today is extra special so Daddy makes everything I love for breakfast. We eat pancakes with banana eyes, strawberry noses, and turkey bacon smiles.

Mama calls the party I am going to tonight an awards show.

And because the party is glamorous, someone has come to our house to do my hair.

My sister and I watch in awe as she works her magic.

And when she finishes . . .
my hair
is
beautiful—

no matter what my big brother says.

Next I get to put on my dress.

It is beautiful too.

I twirl in front of the mirror in
my blue dress that perfectly matches my shoes.

Mama says at the awards show there will be lots of people and flashing cameras.

Daddy reminds me to just smile and think of my favorite things.

My baby
brother gives
me a flower.

Then everyone waves us away.

Waiting outside
is the fanciest car
I've ever seen.

Mama and I sing loudly to the radio

and wave at people through the sunroof.

As we get closer, I hear the roars
of fans and see the flashing of lights.
We're here!

and
I fall
on
my
face.

I think of pancakes with my sister and brothers.
I think of Scruffy by my side.

I think of Daddy.

Then I smile.

There is no
tap,
tap,
tapping in blue shoes on the red carpet.

Mama and I pose for photos as we walk.

At first
I'm shy . . .

but then
I relax

and get into it.

Inside, a nice man gives me snacks, someone else moves so I can see, and Mama whispers funny things in my ear.

The whole place sparkles, and even though the party is looooong, I'm having the time of my life.

I don't win, but Mama and I have
ice cream sundaes just the same
and then giggle all the way home.

The house is asleep when we get there,
and Mama says I should be too.

But I get out of bed
and
   tap,
     tap,
       tap
to the hall window
to watch the stars
twinkling in the sky.

Mama calls out,
"Who's that?"
"It's just me, Mama,"
I say. "It's just me."